Dear Dragon's Fun With Shapes

by Margaret Hillert

Illustrated by David Schimmell

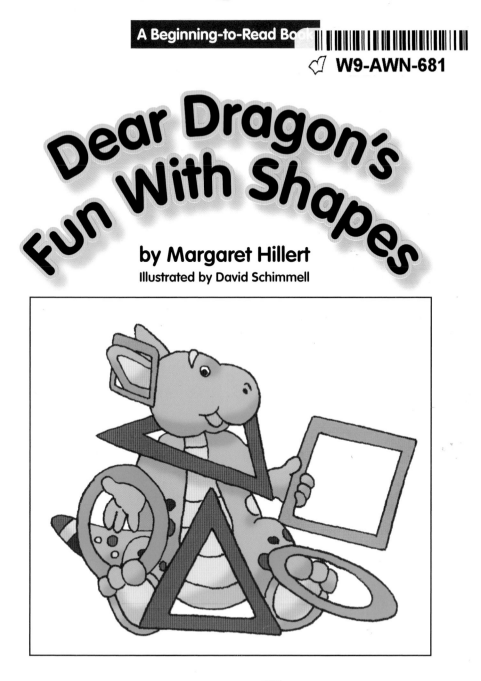

NORWOOD HOUSE PRESS

The **Dear Dragon** series is comprised of carefully written books that extend the collection of classic readers you may remember from your own childhood. Each book features text focused on common sight words. Through the use of controlled text, these books provide young children with abundant practice recognizing the words that appear most frequently in written text. Rapid recognition of high-frequency words is one of the keys for developing automaticity which, in turn, promotes accuracy and rate necessary for fluent reading. The many additional details in the pictures enhance the story and offer opportunities for students to expand oral language and develop comprehension.

Shannon Cannon

Shannon K. Cannon, Ph.D.
Literacy Consultant

Norwood House Press • P.O. Box 316598 • Chicago, Illinois 60631
For more information about Norwood House Press please visit our website at
www.norwoodhousepress.com or call 866-565-2900.

Text copyright ©2013 by Margaret Hillert. Illustrations and cover design
copyright ©2013 by Norwood House Press, Inc. All rights reserved. No part of
this book may be reproduced or utilized in any form or by any means without
written permission from the publisher.

Paperback ISBN: 978-1-60357-447-1

The Library of Congress has cataloged the original hardcover edition with the
following call number: 2012012628

Printed in ShenZhen, Guangdong, China.
287R–102015.

Cookies, cookies.
I like to work with you Mother.
I like to help make cookies.

Cookies have shapes.
This one is a circle.

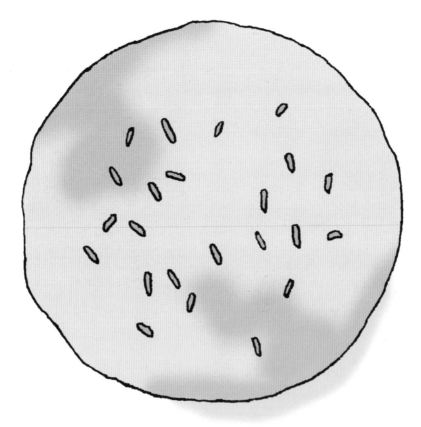

The red cookie has
a triangle shape.

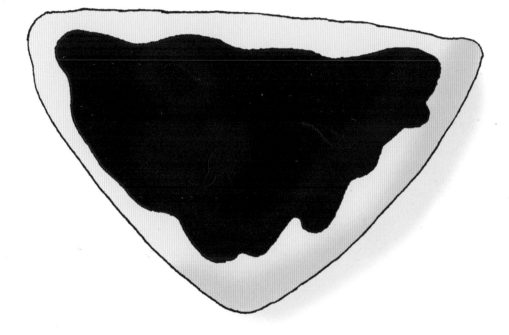

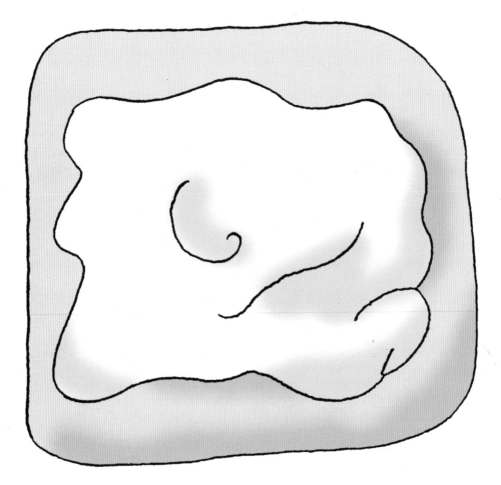

This one is a square.

A dragon has a lot of shapes!

Mother, I see a man
at the door.
Look. Look.

You are good to me.
This makes me happy.

Look Mother.
This is a square box.
Can you guess what is in it?

I will guess there are toys in the box.

Oh, boy!
Oh, boy!
What fun this will be!
See what I can make!

This is like the triangle I play at school.

Now I want to go out and look for shapes.

Here. Here.
Come and eat some circles and triangles.
Then you can go out.

Yes, Mother.
That looks good.

I am on two circles!
And look up there— a triangle.

I can make this circle work.

Look at it go.

And I can walk on these.

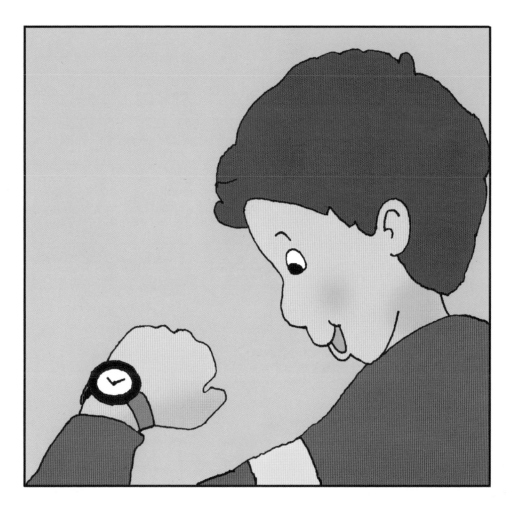

This little circle is a good help to me.

Look up there.
That looks like a circle too.
We have to go in now.

Here you are with me.
And here I am with you.
Oh, what a good day, dear dragon.

WORD LIST

Dear Dragon's Fun With Shapes **uses the 76 words listed below.**
The 4 words bolded below represent the name of shapes and serve as an introduction to new vocabulary, while the other 72 are pre-primer.   You may wish to write the words on index cards and use them to help your child build automatic word recognition. Regular practice with these words will enhance your child's fluency in reading connected text.

a	go	now	that
am	good		the
and	guess	of	then
are		oh	there
at	happy	on	these
	has	one	this
be	have	out	to
box	help		too
boy	here	play	toys
			triangle(s)
can	I	red	two
circle(s)	in		up
come	is	school	
cookie(s)	it	see	walk
		shape(s)	want
day	like	some	we
dear	little	someone	what
door	look(s)	something	who
dragon	lot	**square**	will
			with
eat	make(s)		work
	man		
for	me		yes
fun	mother		you

ABOUT THE AUTHOR

Photograph by Glenna Washburn

Margaret Hillert has written over 80 books for children who are just learning to read. Her books have been translated into many different languages and over a million children throughout the world have read her books. She first started writing poetry as a child and has continued to write for children and adults throughout her life. A first grade teacher for 34 years, Margaret is now retired from teaching and lives in Michigan where she likes to write, take walks in the morning, and care for her three cats.

ABOUT THE ADVISOR

Shannon K. Cannon is a teacher educator, staff developer, and curriculum writer. She earned her doctorate in Language, Literacy, and Culture from the University of California Davis, where she serves on their clinical faculty supervising pre-service teachers, teaching elementary methods courses in reading/language arts and technology, and teaching Master's courses in inquiry. She began her career teaching second grade. She then spent over 15 years in educational publishing where her work included developing and writing curricular programs as well as providing professional development support to classroom teachers.

ABOUT THE ILLUSTRATOR

David Schimmell served as a professional firefighter for 23 years before hanging up his boots and helmet to devote himself to working as an illustrator of children's books. David has happily created illustrations for the New Dear Dragon books as well as the artwork for educational and retail book projects. Born and raised in Evansville, Indiana, he lives there today with his wife and family.